Bank Street

ABOUT THE BANK STREET READY-TO-READ SERIES

More than seventy-five years of educational research, innovative teaching, and quality publishing have earned The Bank Street College of Education its reputation as America's most trusted name in early childhood education.

Because no two children are exactly alike in their development, the Bank Street Ready-to-Read series is written on three levels to accommodate the individual stages of reading readiness of children ages three through eight.

○ *Level 1:* GETTING READY TO READ (Pre-K–Grade 1)
Level 1 books are perfect for reading aloud with children who are getting ready to read or just starting to read words or phrases. These books feature large type, repetition, and simple sentences.

● *Level 2:* READING TOGETHER (Grades 1–3)
These books have slightly smaller type and longer sentences. They are ideal for children beginning to read by themselves who may need help.

○ *Level 3:* I CAN READ IT MYSELF (Grades 2–3)
These stories are just right for children who can read independently. They offer more complex and challenging stories and sentences.

All three levels of The Bank Street Ready-to-Read books make it easy to select the books most appropriate for your child's development and enable him or her to grow with the series step by step. The levels purposely overlap to reinforce skills and further encourage reading.

We feel that making reading fun is the single most important thing anyone can do to help children become good readers. We hope you will become part of Bank Street's long tradition of learning through sharing.

The Bank Street College of Education

For a free color catalog describing Gareth Stevens' list of high-quality books and
multimedia programs, call 1-800-542-2595 (USA) or 1-800-461-9120 (Canada).
Gareth Stevens Publishing's Fax: (414) 225-0377.
See our catalog, too, on the World Wide Web: http://gsinc.com

Library of Congress Cataloging-in-Publication Data

Orgel, Doris.
    Button soup / by Doris Orgel; illustrated by Pau Estrada.
       p. cm. -- (Bank Street ready-to-read)
    Summary: In this modern version of the French folktale "Stone Soup," Rag-Tag Meg shows
the neighborhood how to make a delicious pot of soup starting with only water and an old
wooden button.
    ISBN 0-8368-1761-3 (lib. bdg.)
    [1. Folklore--France.] I. Estrada, Pau., ill. II. Title. III. Series.
PZ8.1.O59Bu 1998
398.2'0944--dc21   97-28944

This edition first published in 1998 by
Gareth Stevens Publishing
1555 North RiverCenter Drive, Suite 201
Milwaukee, Wisconsin 53212 USA

Printed in Mexico

1 2 3 4 5 6 7 8 9 02 01 00 99 98

Bank Street Ready-to-Read™

BUTTON SOUP

by Doris Orgel
Illustrated by Pau Estrada

A Byron Preiss Book

Gareth Stevens Publishing
MILWAUKEE

One day, outside the corner store,
this woman came up to us.
She said, "I'm Rag-Tag Meg,
   and I'm hungry."
"Sorry," my grandpa told her.

I felt bad—we had all this stuff
and she had nothing.
"Don't you worry," said Rag-Tag Meg,
and she walked away.

When we got home
I felt kind of lonesome.
I looked out the window.

Then Rag-Tag Meg came strolling by.
She smiled and waved to me.
"I'm going outside, Grandpa."
He nodded and went to sleep.

We walked around together.
Suddenly she picked up an old button.
"Hey, look!"
She got all happy,
like it was made of gold.

Then in a junk pile she saw
a big old iron pot and spoon.
She grabbed them.
"Just what we need!"

We washed the pot and spoon.
We put water in the pot
and Meg built a fire under it.
I didn't know what for, but it was fun.

Then Meg hopped up on the fountain
and shouted loud as bells,
"Anyone who's hungry,
come on out!
I'm cooking button soup!"

People came and looked in the pot.
"Nothing in there but water!"
They laughed and made fun of Meg.
But she was singing:
"Button, button, made of wood,
make some soup, and make it good."

She dropped the button in the pot.
People said mean things, like
"Who ever heard of button soup?"
"She's crazy, she's a nut case."

I stood up for Meg.
"This soup will be great," I said.
"It just needs a little—"
But I couldn't think what.

Meg was nodding, stirring, singing,
"Button, button in the pot,
can a little help a lot?"
I thought of my mom—
how she used to make soup.
And I said, "It needs a little parsley
and dill."

The grown-ups just laughed.
But this boy Stevie, from up the block,
said, "Parsley and dill, we have those!"
And he brought some.

Meg let him drop them in.
And she sang,
*"Dill and parsley in the pot,
will they help the soup a lot?"*
And great big bubbles came up.

"The button says yes," said Meg,
like she could hear it.
"But it wishes it had a few onions."

The grown-ups laughed like anything.
But a girl with braids said,
"We have onions."
And she brought some.
Meg plopped them in.
Mm, it started smelling good.

Even the grown-ups could smell it.
The lady from the cleaning store
brought some celery to put in.
Mr. Wong brought noodles.
And Mrs. McGonigal from next door
brought soup bones, greens, and beans.

Old Mr. Brown brought a carrot.
Meg grinned and sang really loud,
"Button, button made of wood,
now this soup is getting good!"
And tons of bubbles came up.

The soup smelled better and better.
"But something is still missing,"
I whispered to Meg.
She nodded, like she knew.

I ran home.
Grandpa woke up from snoring.
"Where have you been?"
"Come see," I said.

I dashed in the kitchen
and grabbed our chicken.
I dragged Grandpa out the door.

Meg cheered and called me by my name.
"Yea, Mandy!"
I got really glad.
I plopped the chicken in the pot,
and it went "Glug,"
like "Thank you."

The smell got wonderful.
People said, "Mmmm!"—even the ones
who made mean jokes before.
Mr. Wong brought bowls and spoons
from his noodle shop.
He brought a big ladle, too.

Meg dished out the soup.
You should have been there!

We all had seconds.
Meg and I had thirds.
We never tasted soup that good!

When the pot was nearly empty,
Meg scooped out the button.
She gave it a kiss.

Then she threw it in the air.
I watched it go way, way high.
And when I turned back,
Meg was gone, whoosh,
just like that.
But you know what?

I still have that button.
I'll keep it all my life.